Happy!

Nancy Carlson

Carolrhoda Books Minneapolis · New York

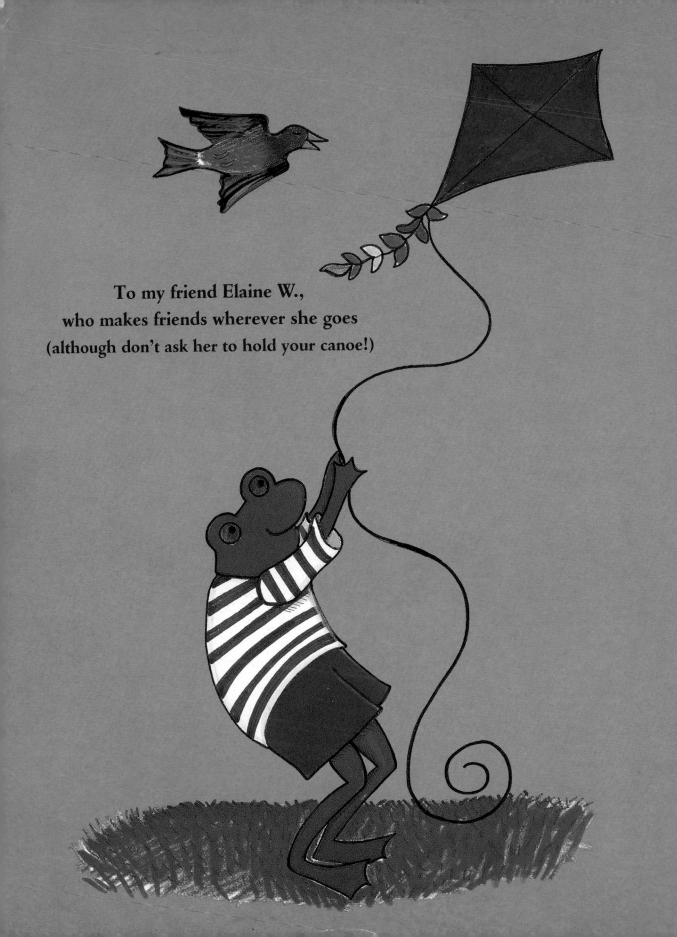

To my friend Elaine W.,
who makes friends wherever she goes
(although don't ask her to hold your canoe!)

Feeling sad? Cheer up! Life is a lot more fun when you **think happy!**

So make yourself happy by looking in the mirror and shouting, **"I AM COOL!"**

Wear those flashy socks and be
the first kid in school to

play the bagpipes.

Make Yourself
Happy
by speaking up for yourself!

When you can't figure something out,

ask for help.

If a **bully** is bothering you,

remember there is **always** someone to help you.

Make Yourself

Happy

by having fun!

Play outside until **dark**.

Throw a **party** or…

put on a
show.

Make Yourself **Happy**

by taking care of your body!

Go for a **bike ride.**

Get a **good night's** sleep.

Drink lots of water because
your body **LOVES** it!

Make Yourself **Happy**

by being friendly!

Wave at your neighbors and guess what?

They'll wave back!

Accept hugs from people who care about you.

And hug them back, because

HUGS JUST FEEL GOOD!

Be the first to say hi to the new kid and ...

...you might find a **new friend**.

Listen to old folks because they have **great stories** to tell!

Make Yourself Happy

by staying calm.

Have **faith** and you'll always have
someone to talk to.

Think happy thoughts when things are tough.

When you don't feel lovable,

you'll make everyone around you
happy too!